MW00911493

MY BIBLE STORYBOOK
IS PRESENTED TO:

Kim and alyssa

ON THIS DATE:

6-5-05

PRESENTED BY:

clare Vaught
nowen as
al50 momy!

Author's Note: This book contains quotes from the King James Version of the Bible. They are characterized in italic print. Quotes not in italic print are used for continuity of the story line.

ISBN 1-55517-496-5

v.1

Published and Distributed by:

925 North Main, Springville, UT 84663 • 801/489-4084

CFI

Publishing and Distribution Since 1986

Cedar Fort, Incorporated

CFI Distribution • CFI Books • Council Press • Bonneville Books

Typeset and Page Layout by Lyle V. Mortimer

Printed in the United States of America

For my husband Dean

Thank you for your unwavering support and for making all my dreams come true!

Acknowledgments

I would like to thank several generous and talented people for their involvement in the completion of this storybook. Thank you to my "Tokyo" friends, Joyce Thompson, Lynell Nielson and Stephanie Conlee. Your time and expertise is greatly appreciated and each of you helped in making this a very special storybook.

Thank you to my husband Dean, for all of your time spent proofreading this text and for your love of Top Ramen!

Thank you to my daughter Amanda, for listening to the stories and suggesting some of your favorites. Look on page 16 for *A Perfect City* and on page 26 for *A Pillar of Salt*.

Thank you to my son Ryan, for your artistic drawings. Look for your animals on pages 5, 20, 22, 23, 96 and 118.

And thank you to my little buddy Sean for hearing the stories and showing so much enthusiasm!

And finally, thank you to Lyle Mortimer and the staff at CFI for your continued support.

My Bible Storybook

Favorite Bible Stories

As Told and Illustrated by
Laura Lee Rostrom

CONTENTS

IN THE BEGINNING

A long, long time ago, Heavenly Father asked Jesus to create heaven and earth. Jesus created them in six days. On the first day, He divided the darkness from the light. The darkness He called night. The light He called day. And He saw that the light was good.

On the second day, Jesus created the firmament. He called it heaven. Heaven has lots of bright, shining stars and planets of many sizes.

The Lord created the dry land on the third day. He divided the land from the waters. He called the dry land, earth. And He called the waters, sea. He made all types of beautiful plants and delicious fruit trees on the earth. And He saw that this was good.

On the fourth day, Jesus created two great lights. The bright, warm sun to lighten the day and the glowing moon to lighten the night.

On the fifth day, Jesus created wondrous whales and swift-moving sharks along with all other sea life. He also created all types of birds, which fly high in the sky. Then Jesus blessed the fish and the birds.

On the sixth day, Jesus created all living creatures to dwell on the earth. He created tall giraffes and playful monkeys. He created fierce tigers and cuddly kittens. And when Jesus saw that all He made was good, He created a man called Adam. Man was created in God's image. Adam's sons and daughters would use and care for this new, beautiful earth.

The Lord rested from all His work on the seventh day. This was a special day and He blessed it. We call this day the Sabbath day.

Genesis 1-2

ADAM AND EVE

The Lord planted a beautiful garden on His new Earth. It had lots of colorful flowers and various fruit trees. He called it the Garden of Eden. Adam cared for the garden and he named all the living creatures.

But the Lord did not like Adam being alone. So He caused Adam to fall into a deep sleep. He took a rib from Adam and made a woman. Adam called her Eve. He was happy to have a friend and wife. Together they could care for the garden and be happy.

Genesis 2-3

THE GARDEN OF EDEN

The Garden of Eden had many delicious fruit trees. Adam and Eve were free to eat any fruit in the garden, except one. That was the fruit of a special tree. The Lord called it the tree of knowledge of good and evil. If Adam and Eve ate from this tree, they would have to leave the beautiful garden.

One day, a serpent who was Satan, asked Eve to eat the fruit of this special tree. The fruit looked delicious. Eve did eat. She gave some to Adam, too.

Later on, God called Adam. Adam and Eve were frightened. They knew they should not have eaten from this special tree. They also saw that they were naked. They tried to hide from God.

God asked Adam if he had eaten the fruit from the special tree. Adam said, “Eve gave me the fruit of the tree, and I did eat.”

Then God asked Eve, "What have you done"? Eve said, "The serpent told me to eat, and I did eat."

God scolded and cursed the serpent. It would have to crawl on its belly from then on. And Adam and Eve were told to leave the beautiful garden. When Adam and Eve left the garden, they were sad that they had made a mistake. But now they would make a new home and soon start their family.

Genesis 3

A PERFECT CITY

Many years after Adam and Eve left the Garden of Eden, lots of people lived on the earth. They were all related to Adam and Eve. One relative was Enoch. Enoch was a prophet. The Lord would visit Enoch and walk and talk with him.

Enoch was a righteous man and he taught everyone in his city to live righteously too. Because all the people living in his city were so good, one day the Lord brought the whole city up to heaven to live with Him. Enoch, the people and everything in the city moved up to heaven!

Genesis 5

NOAH AND THE ARK

Long ago lived a prophet named Noah. The Lord was pleased with Noah and his family.

But the Lord was not pleased with anyone else. They were all doing bad things. God wanted to start over. So He asked Noah to build an ark. An ark is a gigantic boat that can carry people and lots of animals.

The Lord told Noah to collect two of every animal, both male and female. Noah collected elephants and lions and koala bears. He collected turtles and goats and llamas. Then God caused it to rain really hard for forty days and forty nights. The whole earth was covered with water.

Noah and his family were safe in the ark. The animals were safe, too.

One day, Noah let a dove fly away to see if there was dry land. But the dove returned when it could not find any. Then later on Noah let the dove fly away again. This time it returned with an olive leaf. Noah let the dove fly away a third time. This time when it did not come back Noah knew they could land the ark soon and start a new life.

God placed a colorful rainbow in the sky. He promised to never destroy mankind again. We can remember this promise whenever we see a colorful rainbow in the sky.

Genesis 6-9

ABRAHAM AND SARAH

Long ago lived a prophet named Abraham. Abraham and his wife wanted to have a child. But Sarah was too old to have a child. Then one day three holy men came to visit Abraham. They told him that Sarah would bear a son. Sarah overheard the holy men talking outside the tent. She laughed to herself. How could she, an old woman, bear a child?! But the holy men replied, *"Is anything too hard for the Lord?"*

And Sarah, in her old age, did bear a healthy son. Sarah and Abraham named their new son, Isaac. They were very happy to finally have a child.

Genesis 18, 21 (Genesis 18:14)

A PILLAR OF SALT

In Abraham's lifetime, there were two great cities. They were called Sodom and Gomorrah. God was not pleased with the people living in these two cities. The people were selfish and wicked.

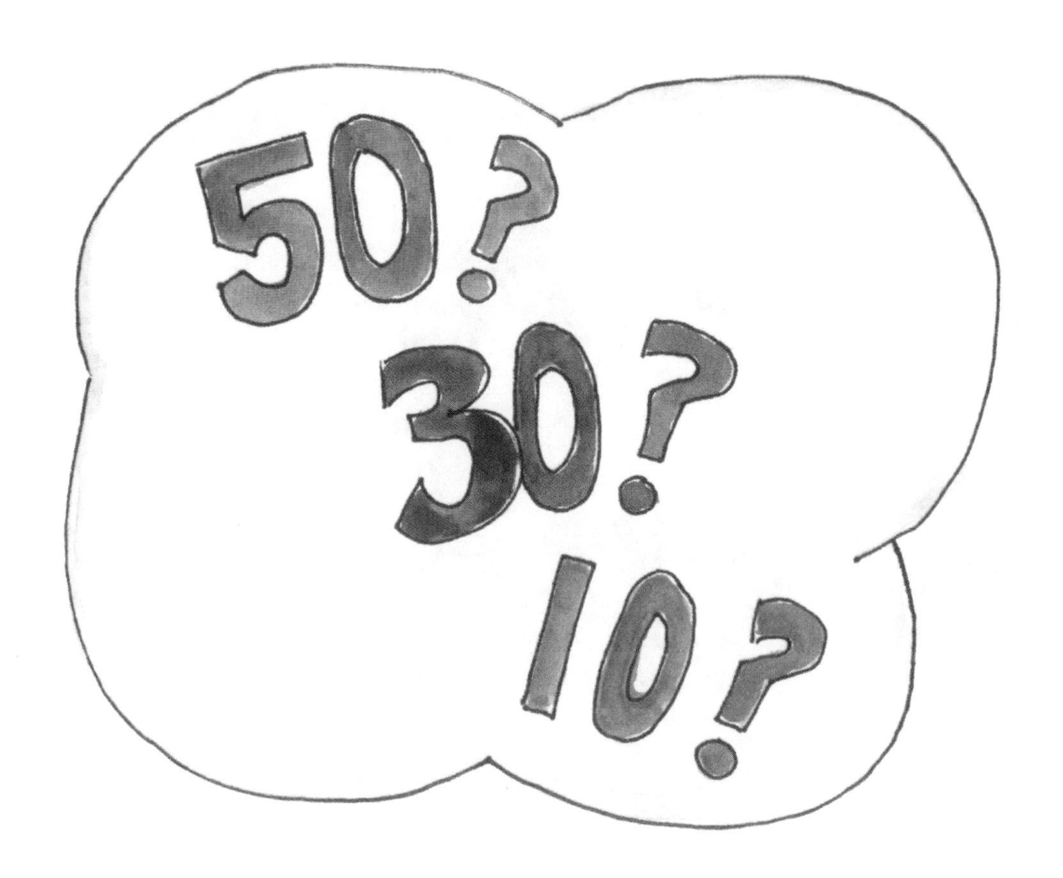

Abraham did not want God to destroy the cities. He asked God, "If there are fifty righteous people living in the cities, will you save them?" God replied, "If there are fifty righteous people, I will save them." Then Abraham asked, "If there are thirty righteous people, will you save them?" God replied, "Yes."

Then Abraham continued, “If there are only ten righteous people, will you save the cities?” God answered, “If there are ten righteous people, I will save them.” But there were not even ten righteous people. There were only four righteous people who lived in Sodom.

Abraham's nephew Lot, and his wife and their two daughters were the only good people. Holy men came to them and said, "You must leave your city and never look back or else you will die."

After Lot and his family left their city, God caused fire and brimstone to rain. It rained on Sodom and Gomorrah and destroyed all the wicked people.

Lot's wife was very curious. She knew she should not look back. But she looked over her shoulder anyway. When she did, her body turned into a pillar of salt! Lot and his two daughters did not look back. They ran away and were safe.

Genesis 18-19

ABRAHAM AND ISAAC

Sarah and Abraham loved their only son, Isaac, very much. Abraham taught Isaac many things. He taught him how to offer burnt offerings to God. This was an important custom to Abraham and his people.

One day the Lord asked Abraham to offer his only son, Isaac, as a burnt offering. Abraham felt very sad to be asked to do this, but he trusted God. Abraham and Isaac traveled to a far away mountain. Abraham prepared an altar on the third day. He tied up Isaac and laid him upon the wood.

Just as Abraham was about to sacrifice his only son, an angel of God called from heaven. The angel stopped Abraham and said, “Now I know you will obey God.” He said Isaac could go free.

Then Abraham looked up and saw a ram stuck in a bush. He let Isaac go and together they gave the ram as a burnt offering. They were very grateful that Isaac's life was spared and that God provided them with a different offering.

Genesis 22

REBEKAH'S FAITH

When Isaac was old enough to marry, his father helped him find a wife. Abraham asked a trusted servant to go back to their homeland and bring back a wife for Isaac.

The servant was nervous. He wondered, “How will I choose the right wife for Isaac?” But the servant had faith that the Lord would help him.

When the servant arrived at the city of Nahor, he saw a well. He prayed to God and asked Him, "Please God, give me a sign so I will know who to choose for Isaac's wife. Please have her offer me a drink from this well. Then have her give water to all of my camels, as well."

Just then a beautiful woman came to the well. She offered a drink of well water to the servant. He humbly took the drink. Then she drew water for all ten of his camels.

The servant was so excited! He knew this was a sign from God. The woman's name was Rebekah. Her family knew Abraham. The servant asked Rebekah if she would leave her family and marry Isaac.

Rebekah had tremendous faith. She believed God wanted her to leave and marry Isaac. So Rebekah left her family and went with the servant. Isaac was grateful that the Lord helped the servant find Rebekah. From the first moment Isaac saw her, he loved Rebekah with all his heart.

Genesis 24

A SPECIAL BLESSING

Isaac and Rebekah had twin sons. Esau was the oldest. Jacob was the youngest. When Isaac became very old, he wanted to bless his sons. He called for his oldest son, Esau. He told Esau to prepare a feast for them. Isaac would give Esau an important blessing after they ate.

But Rebekah overheard Isaac's conversation. She believed their youngest son, Jacob, should receive the firstborn blessing, not Esau. She remembered that one day when Esau was very hungry he told Jacob he would sell his birthright to Jacob for a bowl of pottage. Rebekah knew that Esau really did not value his firstborn birthright.

So Rebekah quickly prepared Isaac's favorite foods. She sent Jacob to meet with his father. Esau had lots of hair on his arms. So Jacob covered his arms so they would feel hairy, like his brother Esau.

Isaac could not see. So he asked Jacob, "Are you Esau?" Jacob said, "Yes, I am." Isaac asked to feel his arms. When they felt hairy, Isaac believed it was Esau. They enjoyed a big meal together.

Isaac gave Jacob an important blessing when they finished eating. He said to Jacob, "You will inherit all of my land. And someday you will be the father of many children and grandchildren. Many great rulers and kings will come from your family." Jacob understood the importance of this blessing. He was grateful he received it from his father.

Esau was furious when he learned that Jacob received the first-born blessing. Rebekah sent Jacob away so Esau could not hurt him. Jacob left his family and traveled to his mother's homeland to start a new life.

Genesis 27

JACOB'S SURPRISE

Jacob met his uncle Laban when he traveled to his mother's homeland. Then Jacob met Laban's daughters. His oldest daughter was Leah. His younger daughter was Rachel. Jacob fell in love with Rachel. Jacob asked Laban if he could work seven years for him, to earn Rachel as his wife. Laban agreed to this arrangement.

A wedding was planned after seven years. Jacob thought he was marrying Rachel. But after the wedding, he took off her veil and saw that it was not Rachel. It was Rachel's older sister, Leah! Jacob was shocked. Laban had tricked him! Laban said, "It is not our custom to marry the younger daughter before the older daughter, so you need to marry Leah first."

In those days a man could have more than one wife. So Laban told Jacob that he could marry Rachel too, but he would need to stay and work another seven years. Jacob loved Rachel very much. So he agreed to marry Rachel and work another seven years. Jacob was truly happy when he married Rachel.

Genesis 29

A FAMILY REUNION

The Lord told Jacob to move his family back to his childhood homeland when he had many children. Jacob hoped his brother, Esau, would not be angry with him. He brought gifts for his brother.

Esau was not angry with Jacob anymore. In fact, he was filled with joy when he saw Jacob returning. He ran to meet him. They hugged for a long time. They were so happy to be together again. Jacob introduced his new family to Esau. Esau asked them to stay. They could live anywhere in the land.

Genesis 33

A NEW NAME

Isaac's blessing to Jacob was beginning to come true. Jacob had a large family and lots of land. God visited Jacob. He said, "I will not call you Jacob anymore, but I will call you Israel, for you will be the father of great nations, and kings will be born into your family."

Israel had a daughter, Dinah, and twelve sons. Their names were Reuben, Simeon, Levi, Judah, Issachar, Zebulun, Dan, Naphtali, Gad, Asher, and from his beloved Rachel, came Joseph and Benjamin.

Genesis 30-35

JOSEPH'S COLORFUL COAT

Of all his children, Israel loved Joseph the best. Israel gave Joseph a special gift. It was a handsome coat made with many colors. Joseph loved wearing his new coat. He wore it when he watched the flocks. And he wore it when he played with his brothers.

His brothers felt jealous. They wished Joseph would not wear his colorful coat. It reminded them of how much their father loved Joseph. And they also did not like Joseph's dreams.

In one dream, Joseph and his brothers looked like sheaves of grain. He was standing straight but his brothers were all bowing down to him. And in another dream, Joseph saw the sun, the moon and eleven stars bowing to him. His brothers did not like the thought of bowing down to Joseph.

One day, Joseph's father, Israel, asked Joseph to meet his brothers in a far away place. Joseph's brothers made a plan to get rid of Joseph. They sold him as a slave. He was taken away to Egypt. When their father asked what happened to Joseph, his older brothers made up a story. They told their father that a wild beast had killed Joseph.

Israel was heartbroken! He did not think he could bear to lose his son Joseph. He believed his older sons' story that Joseph had died and he wept.

Genesis 30-37

JOSEPH IN EGYPT

Joseph's master in Egypt was a fair man. He treated Joseph well. Joseph was learning a lot about the Egyptians. He was a good worker.

But his master's wife was not good to him. She liked teasing Joseph. Joseph tried to stay away from her. But one day she wanted him to do something he knew was wrong. He told her, "No!" But that made her angry and she got him into trouble. He had to go to an Egyptian prison.

Joseph made many friends in prison. Everyone really liked him. Two of his friends were the Pharaoh's personal butler and baker. One night they each had a dream they did not understand. God gave Joseph the talent to interpret dreams. So Joseph told them what their dreams meant.

Joseph explained the butler's dream. He said, "You will be getting out of prison in three days. And you will return to serve Pharaoh." Joseph then asked the butler to remember him so that Joseph could get out of prison, too. In three days, the butler did get out of prison, just as Joseph said. But the butler did not remember to help Joseph.

Genesis 40

PHARAOH'S DREAM

One night the great Pharaoh of Egypt had a strange dream. He wondered what it meant. He asked his advisers, but they did not understand the dream. When Pharaoh's butler heard of the strange dream, he remembered Joseph in prison. The butler told Pharaoh about him. Pharaoh sent for Joseph. He asked Joseph to explain his strange dream.

In his dream, Pharaoh saw seven fat cows that were eaten by seven thin cows. But the thin cows did not get bigger from eating the fat cows. Then he saw seven full ears of corn on one stalk. But seven thin corn stalks overtook the fat corn stalks and they blew away.

Joseph understood Pharaoh's dream. He told Pharaoh there would be seven years of good harvest. They would have an abundance of food and livestock. But the following seven years would bring famine. Egypt's crops would not grow and their cows and goats would die without food to eat.

Joseph told Pharaoh to choose a wise leader to save grain during the seven prosperous years. Then Egypt would be prepared for the seven years of famine.

Pharaoh was grateful to Joseph. He was the only person who understood his strange dream. He asked Joseph to save grain for the next seven years. Pharaoh made Joseph a leader and ruler over all the land. Pharaoh gave Joseph fine clothing and jewelry and a chariot to ride on. All the Egyptians bowed down to Joseph.

Genesis 41

SEVEN GOOD YEARS

Joseph married Asenath. They had two sons, Manasseh and Ephraim. It was Joseph's responsibility to save grain and prepare for the famine. This was a very happy time for Joseph.

Genesis 41

JOSEPH RULES OVER ALL THE LAND

When the famine came, it was Joseph's job to sell corn to the people who were hungry. One day, ten men came from the land of Canaan to buy corn. They were all brothers. Joseph recognized them. They were his brothers! But they did not recognize Joseph.

Joseph remembered his earlier dreams. They were being fulfilled. His brothers were all bowing down to him. Joseph did not want his brothers to leave. He made a plan to keep his brothers in Egypt.

Joseph accused his brothers of being spies. He said he would only sell them corn if they brought back their youngest brother, Benjamin. Joseph used to play with Benjamin when they were little. Joseph missed Benjamin very much. Joseph kept one brother in Egypt. The other brothers returned to Canaan to get Benjamin.

Genesis 42

JOSEPH'S REUNION

Israel did not want his youngest son, Benjamin, to go to Egypt. But he saw there was no other way. His family would starve without corn to eat. So Benjamin went with his brothers to Egypt.

Joseph invited his brothers to eat at his home. The brothers were frightened. They thought they had done something wrong. But Joseph was kind to them and they enjoyed the comforts of Joseph's home.

Joseph did not want them to leave so he placed a silver cup in Benjamin's bag. When his brothers were leaving the city, guards stopped them. They said Joseph was missing a silver cup from his house. Whoever had the silver cup would have to stay and be a servant to Joseph. Benjamin was surprised when the guards found the silver cup in his bag! He did not put it there.

Benjamin's brothers begged Joseph to let him go. They told Joseph it would break their father's heart if his youngest son did not return. Joseph could not hide his feelings any longer. He told them that he was their brother, Joseph. They could hardly believe him.

At first they were frightened. They thought Joseph would be angry with them because they had sold him as a slave. But Joseph was not angry. He was so happy to see his family again! Joseph hugged each brother. They held each other and cried for joy! He told them he was not mad at them. He said, "Now I know it was God's plan to bring me to Egypt."

Genesis 42-45

ISRAEL MOVES TO EGYPT

Joseph asked his brothers to return to Canaan. He asked them to bring their father and move to Egypt. Pharaoh gave them a home. And they would have all the food they needed.

Israel could hardly believe his son Joseph was still alive. He moved his family to Egypt. He and Joseph were so happy to be reunited. They hugged each other for a long time. They were grateful that God brought them back together again.

Genesis 46

THE ISRAELITES

For many years after Israel's death, his family grew and grew. They lived in Egypt and were called Israelites. The Egyptians did not like the Israelites so they made them slaves. The Israelites had to work very hard. They built beautiful buildings and statues for Pharaoh.

The Israelites prayed to God. They asked Him for freedom. God heard their prayers. He sent a prophet named Moses to free them from the Egyptians.

Exodus 1

BABY MOSES

A healthy baby boy was born to an Israelite family. Pharaoh feared the Israelites because there were so many of them. So he commanded all Israelite baby boys to be thrown into the river.

One baby boy was saved. His mother did not throw him in the river. She kept him safe for three months, and then she built a small boat. She placed her baby son in it and put it in the river. The baby boy's older sister followed the boat.

An Egyptian servant found the baby and the boat floating in the river. She brought the boat to the daughter of Pharaoh. When she saw the cute baby boy inside, she decided to keep him. She said she would raise him as her own son.

The baby's sister, who had been following the boat, asked Pharaoh's daughter if she needed someone to care for her new baby. Pharaoh's daughter said she did. So the baby's real mother came to care for her baby son. Pharaoh's daughter named the little baby boy, Moses.

Exodus 1-2

AN EGYPTIAN PRINCE

Moses was raised as an Egyptian. He was a little prince in the Pharaoh's family. He grew to be a fine young man. His older brother would someday be the Pharaoh. Moses enjoyed his life as a prince. He had all the comforts an Egyptian could dream of. But one day his whole life changed. That was the day he learned that he was really an Israelite, and not an Egyptian.

It made Moses sad to see how cruel the Egyptians were to his brothers, the Israelites. One day he saw an Egyptian beating an Israelite slave. Moses tried to stop the Egyptian but in doing this, Moses killed the Egyptian. Moses was scared. He ran away from Egypt.

Exodus 2 •

THE CHOSEN ONE

Moses ran away to a land called Midian. In Midian, he helped seven sisters care for their sheep. He married one of the sisters, Zipporah, and they had a son.

One day when Moses was watching the sheep, he saw a burning bush. Moses was astonished! The bush burned a lot but it did not burn to the ground. The flame kept burning and burning.

Then Moses heard the Lord's voice. He called Moses by name. The Lord asked Moses to take off his shoes. Then the Lord talked to Moses. He said he wanted Moses to help the Israelites get away from the mean Egyptians.

Moses did not know how to do this but the Lord said he would help him. The Lord gave Moses special power and a spokesman. Moses' Israelite brother, Aaron, met Moses in the desert. Together they would free the Israelites.

Exodus 4

LET MY PEOPLE GO

Aaron, Moses and his family traveled to Egypt. Aaron told the Israelites that Moses was going to help them. The Israelites were happy that someone was coming to free them.

Moses and Aaron went to see Pharaoh. Moses said, "Let my people go." But instead of letting the Israelites go, Pharaoh made them work harder. They even had to make bricks without straw, which was very hard.

Then Moses and Aaron went to Pharaoh again. Moses said, "Let my people go." Moses showed Pharaoh God's power. Moses turned his walking stick into a snake. Pharaoh was not impressed. His magicians did the same trick. But then Moses' snake swallowed all of the magicians' snakes. Still Pharaoh would not let the Israelites go.

The following day Moses said, "Let my people go." But Pharaoh again refused. So God turned the river and all their drinking water into blood. All of the fish died and the city smelt very bad. But Pharaoh still would not let the Israelites go.

Then God sent frogs, lice and flies to pester the Egyptians. But they did not bother the Israelites. Moses said, “Let my people go.” But Pharaoh still refused.

After that, all of the Egyptians' animals died. Then all of the Egyptian people grew painful boils and blisters all over their bodies. Next, a huge hailstorm came. It brought lightning and thunder, as Egypt had never seen before. Then a thick darkness of locusts covered the land.

The Egyptian people were not happy. Moses asked, "Now will you let my people go?" But Pharaoh still would not let them go.

Exodus 4-10

THE PASSOVER

The Egyptians saw God's great power. But Pharaoh would not free the Israelites. Finally God told Moses, "I will take the firstborn of every Egyptian family."

To protect the Israelites, God told Moses to have them take blood from a lamb and paint it around their front doors. Then God's angel would know to pass over their house and not destroy their firstborn. The Israelites' children would live.

It was a very sad night for the Egyptians. All of the Egyptians' firstborn children died, even Pharaoh's firstborn son. Pharaoh called for Moses in the middle of the night. He said, "I will let your people go." The Israelites hurried. They did not want Pharaoh to change his mind. All the Israelites, old and young, packed their belongings. They followed Moses out of Egypt.

Exodus 11-13

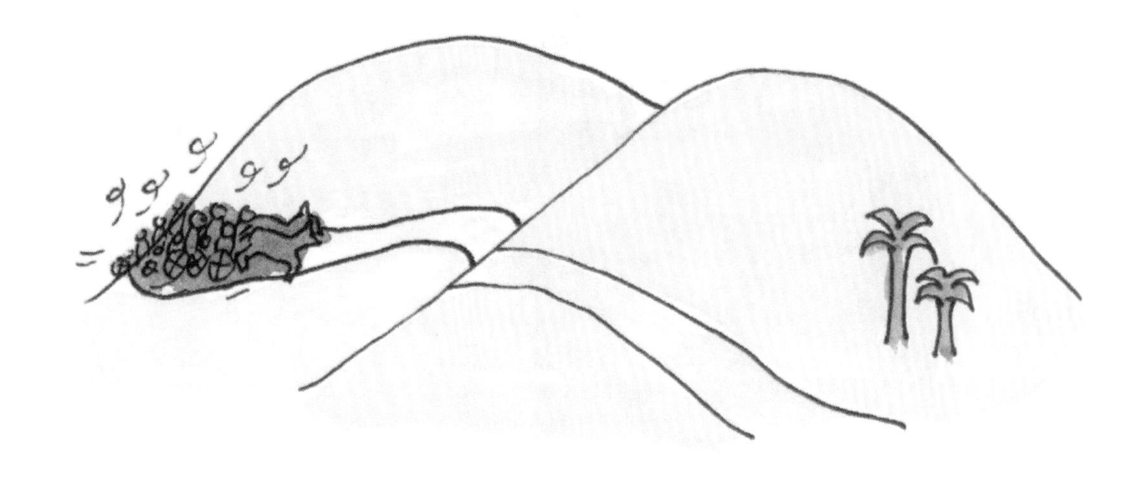

DIVIDING THE RED SEA

Moses and the Israelites traveled away from Egypt. As they came to the Red Sea, they noticed something coming behind them. It was Pharaoh and his soldiers racing towards them in their chariots. Pharaoh had changed his mind! He wanted the Israelites to come back.

The Israelites were trapped. With the Red Sea in front of them and the soldiers coming from behind, they could not get away.

Moses asked God what they should do. God said, "Lift your rod and I will divide the waters of the sea." When Moses did this, the sea divided and the Israelites walked on dry land through the sea. They were able to flee from the Egyptians. The sea closed together after all of the Israelites had crossed. They were so happy to finally be free.

Exodus 16

MANNA SENT FROM HEAVEN

The Israelites followed Moses into the desert. They could not find food to eat, so Moses asked God for help. The Lord sent a type of bread for them to gather and eat. They called the bread, “manna”. Every morning the people gathered enough manna for that day. If they gathered more than they could eat that day, the extra manna would spoil.

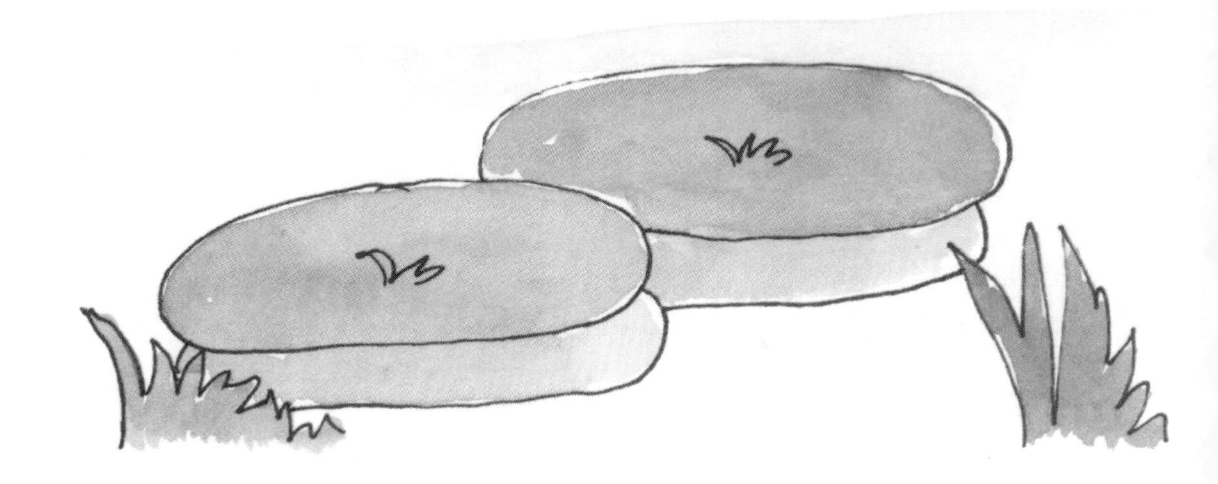

The Lord provided manna every day of the week except for one. The Lord did not send manna on the Sabbath; so the day before, they collected enough manna to last two days and it did not go bad. God gave Moses and his people manna for the next forty years, every day, except on the Sabbath.

Exodus 16

THE TEN COMMANDMENTS

One day Moses went up in a mountain to pray to God. The people were frightened. They saw lightning and heard booming thunder coming from the mountain.

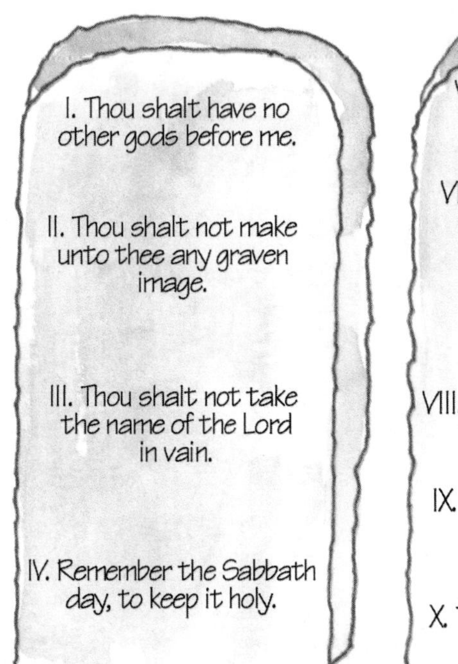

The Lord came to Moses. He said he did not want the Israelites to live like the Egyptians. So God gave Moses the Ten Commandments for his people to follow. These special rules would help the Israelites live in peace. And they would feel happy if they always remembered to follow them.

Exodus 20

JERICHO

After traveling in the wilderness for forty years, the Israelites finally reached their Promised Land. They came to the Land of Canaan. The Lord had promised this land to Abraham and his descendants many years before.

Moses was very old now. He was grateful to see the Promised Land before he died. When Moses died, it was Joshua's turn to lead the Israelites.

The Israelites had a problem when they reached the Promised Land. People were already living there. But the Lord helped them take over many cities. One city was Jericho.

Joshua told the Israelites to march around the city of Jericho every morning for the next six days. After marching each morning the priests blew their horns.

On the seventh day, they marched around Jericho seven times. The last time around they all stopped and the priests blew their horns. Then all the Israelites shouted as loud as they could. When they did this, the city walls came tumbling down!

Joshua 6

JOSHUA

This was an important time for the Israelites. There were twelve groups among the Israelites that came from the twelve sons of Israel. Joshua needed to tell the twelve tribes of Israel where to live. They all divided up into different cities.

Joshua reminded the twelve tribes how good the Lord had been to them. He told them how they escaped from Egypt, and how the Lord brought them to the Promised Land. Joshua told the Israelites they should remember to follow the commandments.

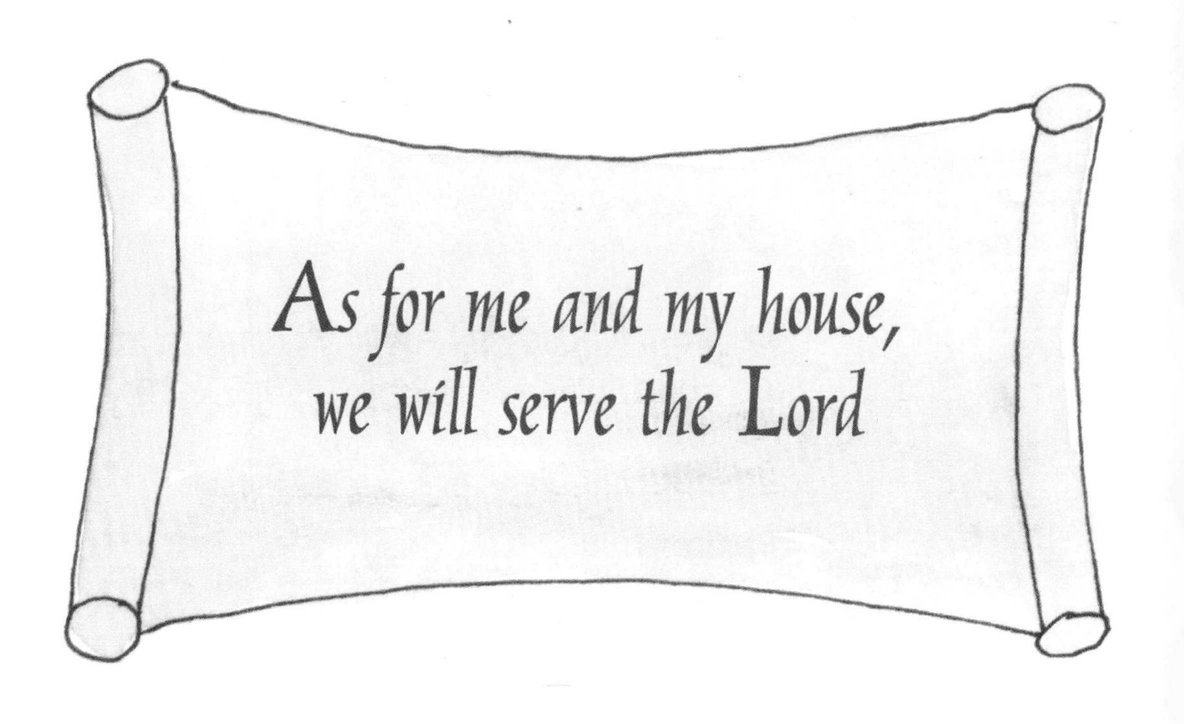

Joshua said, *"Choose you this day whom ye will serve...but as for me and my house, we will serve the Lord."* Joshua hoped all the Israelites would choose to obey God's commandments.

Joshua 13-24 (Joshua 24:15)

SAMSON AND A WILD LION

Long ago an angel appeared to an Israelite woman. He told her that she would bear a special son. Her son would grow to be a strong and courageous man. She named her son Samson. He grew to be the strongest man alive.

One day while Samson was walking through a vineyard, he saw a young lion. The lion gave a loud roar and then jumped on Samson. Samson did not have any weapons. He only had his bare hands. Using only his hands and his great strength, Samson killed the attacking lion.

God told Samson's mother to never cut Samson's hair. As long as Samson did not cut his long hair, God would bless him with great strength.

Judges 13-15

NAOMI AND RUTH

A woman named Naomi lost her husband. A few years later, she lost both of her sons. Her sons' wives were Orpah and Ruth. Naomi told them that they should move back to their parents' home. But Ruth refused to leave Naomi.

Ruth loved Naomi very much and did not want her to be alone. So together they traveled back to Naomi's hometown. An old friend, Boaz, was kind to Naomi and Ruth. With time, Boaz fell in love with Ruth. He asked her to marry him. They had a healthy baby boy.

Ruth was glad to be married again and to have a baby son. She let Naomi help raise her new son. Naomi was so grateful to have such a good friend and a new family.

Ruth 1-4

HANNAH'S COURAGE

Long ago a woman named Hannah was not able to have a child. This made her very sad. She prayed to God. She pleaded, "If you will let me have a son, then I will let a holy priest raise him."

A priest named Eli saw Hannah praying in the temple. He saw how sad she looked. He did not know what she was praying for, but before she left the temple, he told her that the Lord would answer her prayers.

Shortly after, Hannah gave birth to a healthy boy. She was so happy. God had answered her prayers. She named him Samuel. When he was old enough to leave her, she took him to the holy priest, Eli. It must have been very hard for her to say good-bye to her son, but she told Eli that God wanted him to raise Samuel.

Eli was grateful that he was chosen to raise such a special boy. Each year Hannah would make a new coat for Samuel to wear. She and her husband would bring it to the temple where Samuel lived with Eli. Later on, Hannah and her husband had five more children! They were grateful that the Lord had blessed them with three more sons and two daughters to raise.

1 Samuel 1-2

SAMUEL

Samuel was a special boy. People from all over the land knew that someday Samuel would be a prophet. One night the Lord called Samuel while he was sleeping. Samuel thought Eli the Priest was calling him. Samuel went to Eli and said, "Here I am." But Eli said, "I did not call you."

When Samuel returned to his bed, he heard his named called a second time. He returned to Eli, but again Eli said, "I did not call you!"

So Samuel returned to his bed. But again he heard his name called. He went back to Eli. This time Eli told Samuel that it might be the Lord calling him. He said, "If you hear your name called again, answer, 'I hear you, Lord'."

Samuel did hear his name called again. He said, *"Speak; for thy servant heareth."* This was the first time the Lord spoke to Samuel. After this, God spoke to Samuel and helped him guide the Israelites for many, many years.

1 Samuel 3 (1 Samuel 3:10)

A GOOD HEART

One day the Lord asked Samuel to choose a new king for Israel. The Lord told him what to look for in a new king. He said, "*The Lord seeth not as a man seeth; for man looketh on the outward appearance. But the Lord looketh on the heart.*"

The Lord told Samuel to choose one of Jesse's eight sons to be the new king.

Samuel looked at the seven grown brothers. After seeing each one, he knew they were not the right choice. Samuel asked to see the youngest brother. He was in the fields watching the sheep.

When the youngest brother came, Samuel knew that he had a good heart. His name was David. Someday David would be the king of Israel.

1 Samuel 16 (1 Samuel 16: 7)

DAVID AND GOLIATH

One day, when the Israelite and Philistine armies were fighting, a commotion broke out. The Israelites were frightened by one of the Philistine soldiers. They saw a giant man with great strength moving towards them.

The giant was named Goliath. He shouted, “I want to challenge an Israelite. Bring me your best soldier to fight!” But Goliath frightened all of the Israelite soldiers away. They did not want to fight him.

When David brought food to his brothers, he heard about Goliath's challenge. David was only a boy but he asked King Saul if he could fight Goliath. The king thought David was too young. But David said, "I know that God will help me."

The king gave David a breastplate and sword for protection, but David would not use them. He only took his slingshot and five smooth stones.

David went to Goliath. When Goliath saw David coming, he cursed him. He yelled, “Is this the best you can do? Sending a boy to fight me?” But David had faith. He said, “*Thou comest to me with a sword, and with a spear, and with a shield: but I come to thee in the name of the Lord...*”

As Goliath came towards David with his weapons, David pulled out a smooth rock from his bag. He put it in his sling. David swung the slingshot around and around and let the rock go. The rock flew through the sky and hit Goliath right on his forehead. Goliath fell to the ground. Because of David's faith in God, David won! Later David became the king of Israel.

1Samuel 17 (1 Samuel 17:45)

KING SOLOMON

David was a righteous king. When he became too old to rule, he appointed his son, Solomon, to be the new king. Solomon prayed to God. He asked God for wisdom. He wanted to be able to judge his people fairly. God was pleased with Solomon. He granted him more wisdom and knowledge than any other king.

One day, two women came to Solomon. They had each given birth to a child. One child had died during the night and the mother switched the infants while the other mother slept. In the morning the real mother discovered the dead infant. But she knew it was not her son.

The women came to King Solomon asking him to choose the real mother. The mothers would not agree on whose son the child was; so Solomon ordered the child to be cut in half. Each mother could have half of the child.

One woman cried out, “Do not harm the child, it is better that he is raised by the wrong mother. Please, just let him live!” The other woman said only, “Let the king do as he pleases.”

Then King Solomon gave the baby boy to his real mother. He knew the real mother would not want any harm to come to her child. When the people in Solomon's kingdom heard this story, they knew that God was helping him to judge. They were grateful to have such a wise ruler.

1 Kings 3

FED BY RAVENS

There once was a wicked king named Ahab. He wanted the people in his kingdom to worship a statue. He called the statue Baal. The prophet Elijah knew this was wrong. He told the wicked king that they should worship the true God and not a statue. But the king would not listen.

Elijah told the king that the Lord would cause a drought if he did not obey. It would not rain for a long time and the people would not have water to drink. But the king refused. So, the Lord sent the drought.

There was no water to drink but the Lord told Elijah where to find water. He could live near a brook. He could get water from it. Then the Lord sent ravens with food for Elijah to eat.

When the water in the brook dried up, God told Elijah where to live next. He told Elijah to go to a city and look for a woman who was a widow. She would feed him.

At the city gate, Elijah saw a woman gathering sticks. He asked her to feed him. She said, "I only have a little flour and oil to make bread for myself and my son." Elijah promised her that if she made bread for him first, then she would have enough flour and oil to last until the drought ended.

The woman had faith. She believed Elijah. She made his food first. Then she made food for herself and her son. After that, the woman always had flour and oil, just as Elijah promised.

1 Kings 17

ELIJAH

The prophet Elijah stayed with a kind widowed woman and her son in the city. One day the widow's son became very ill. He stopped breathing. The widow was very sad. She did not want her son to die.

The widow found Elijah. She said, “If you are a true prophet, you can bring my son back to life.”

Elijah prayed to God. He asked, "Please give life back to this boy. His mother has been so kind to me. Please let her son live." The Lord heard and answered Elijah's prayer. The boy sat up and smiled at his mother. The widow was so grateful! She thanked Elijah and said, "Now I know you are truly a prophet of God."

1 Kings 17

THE TRUE GOD

Long ago the Lord caused a very bad drought throughout the land. The prophet Elijah hoped this drought would change the wicked king's mind. Elijah wanted the people to worship the true God. But even with the terrible drought, the king would not let the people worship God. He said they must pray to his statue.

Elijah went to see the king. He said, "Let's see which God is true." The king liked this challenge. So Elijah told the king's wicked priests to make an altar. Then Elijah made a different altar. The wicked priests prayed to their statue. They chanted, "Please start a fire on our altar." They chanted all morning. Nothing happened. Then they chanted all afternoon. Still nothing happened.

Then Elijah asked the people watching to pour buckets of water on his stone and wood altar. The people watching were surprised. They knew that wet wood does not burn. But when it was dripping wet with water, Elijah prayed to the true God. He said, *"Hear me, O Lord, hear me, that this people may know that thou art the Lord God...."*

After Elijah said this, a huge ball of fire fell from heaven. It set Elijah's altar on fire! The wood burned, the water burned, and even the stones burned! The people all cheered. They knew that they should only worship the Lord. They knew He was the true God.

1 Kings 18 (I Kings 18:37)

QUEEN ESTHER

Long ago lived a kind and beautiful woman named Esther. She lived in Persia with her cousin Mordecai. Mordecai watched the gate for King Ahasuerus.

King Ahasuerus announced that he wanted to find the most beautiful woman to be his queen. Young ladies from all over Persia came hoping they would be chosen. When Mordecai heard this, he told Esther she should go see the king.

When the king saw Esther, he thought she was the most beautiful of all. He chose her as his new queen. She felt very happy to be chosen.

Esther 1-10

FASTING AND PRAYER

One day, the king's friend, Haman, told the king a lie. He said, "There is a whole group of people in your kingdom who do not obey your rules." Haman asked if he could get rid of these bad people. The king told Haman to do what he thought was best. Then Haman planned for all the Jews in Persia to be destroyed on a certain day.

Mordecai could not believe the king would order such a decree. He cried to God. Esther heard that Mordecai was upset. She sent a servant to find out what was wrong. Mordecai asked Esther to talk to the king. The king did not know that Esther and Mordecai were Jews. They would both have to die because of Haman's cruel plan.

Esther asked her Jewish friends to fast with her. After three days of praying and fasting she went to see the king. She was very nervous. Anyone entering the king's court without being invited might be punished.

When Esther entered the king's court she was relieved to see that the king was happy to see her. Then he asked her what she wanted. She invited him to eat with her. She invited Haman too.

After the king had finished eating, he asked Esther what she wanted. Esther said, "Please let me live!" The king said, "Of course you will live!" But then Esther told him Haman's plan. The king was very angry with Haman. He did not know that Haman wanted to kill all of the Jews.

Esther told the king that she was a Jew. Haman was frightened when he heard this. The king would not allow Haman to follow through with his evil plan. Because of Esther's faith and courage she saved all of her people!

Esther 1-10

JOB

A long time ago, there lived a man named Job. Job was a very righteous man. He had a large family and the most cattle and land of all the people in the East.

One day, Satan asked God, “Can I tempt Job?” The Lord said, “You may, but do not take his life.” Right away a messenger came running to Job. He said, “Some people came and took away all of your cattle and horses. Not one is left.”

Then another messenger came. He said, "Lightning fell from the sky and started a fire. It burned all of your sheep. Not one is left." Then another messenger came. He said, "Some people came and took away all of your camels. Not one is left."

As the last messenger finished talking, another servant came and said, “Job, a strong wind came and blew your house down. All of your children were inside. Not one child is left.”

Job was astonished. He had lost all of his fortune and all of his children at once. He was heart-broken. He fell to the ground and cried out. He said, *"The Lord gave, and the Lord hath taken away."* Job was sad but he never blamed God for his losses.

Job 1-42 (Job 1:21)

JOB IS BLESSED

Later on, Satan caused Job to have painful boils all over his body. The boils made him look very strange. His friends did not even recognize him. Job was sad. But he never blamed God. He asked God to forgive him for his sins.

When the Lord heard this, He blessed Job. He gave him twice as many cattle, sheep and camels as before. Job also had ten more children. His three new daughters were the prettiest in all the land. Job went on to live a long life with more love and wealth than he had before all of his troubles started!

Job 1-42

THE FIERY FURNACE

Once there lived a wicked king named Nebuchadnezzar. King Nebuchadnezzar built a large golden statue. He ordered all the people in his kingdom to worship it. He said, "When you hear my special music playing, you must all bow down and worship my golden statue."

When the king's special music played, all the people in his kingdom bowed down and worshipped the golden statue, except for three men. Shadrach, Meshach and Abed-nego only worshipped the real God. They knew they should not worship a statue.

King Nebuchadnezzar was furious when he heard that three men would not worship his golden statue. He told the three men to come to him. He said, “I will give you one more chance to worship my statue. But if you do not worship it, I will throw you into a fiery furnace.”

Shadrach, Meshach and Abednego answered, "We will never worship a statue. We will only worship the true God."

The king got very angry and ordered them to be thrown into a burning furnace. After the men were put into the furnace the king looked inside. He was surprised! He saw four men walking inside the fiery furnace. One looked like the Son of God. He called to the men.

The three men walked out of the furnace without any burns. They did not even smell of smoke. The king was amazed. He had never seen anything like this before. The Lord protected these men from the fire, because of their courage and unwavering faith.

Daniel 3

DANIEL AND THE LIONS' DEN

There once lived a prophet named Daniel. He helped the king make important decisions. The king also had other men help him. The other men were jealous of Daniel.

They asked the king to make a new law. They said, "You should tell everyone in the kingdom to pray to you." The king liked this idea so he made it a new law.

When Daniel heard the new law, he knew he could not pray to the king. He only prayed to God.

One day, the mean men saw Daniel praying to God. They took him to see the king. They told the king that Daniel was praying to God. He was breaking the king's new law. The king liked Daniel but he could not change his new law. So the mean men threw Daniel into a den with hungry lions. The lions circled Daniel and growled at him really loud.

The king could not sleep during the night. He was so worried about Daniel. He did not want the lions to hurt him. In the morning the king ran to the lions' den.

He called to Daniel, “Are you all right?” Daniel answered, “Yes, I am all right. The Lord closed the lions’ mouths so they could not harm me.” The king and Daniel were both very happy that the Lord had protected him.

Daniel 6

JONAH AND A BIG FISH

There once was a man named Jonah. The Lord asked Jonah to go and preach in a far away city. The city was called Nineveh. Jonah did not want to go. Instead, he decided to run away. Jonah went to a seaport village and boarded a ship.

Soon the ship was tossing to and fro. A huge storm surrounded the ship. The people on board wondered why God caused such a big storm. They drew lots to see whom God was angry with. It was Jonah.

They tried to row the ship to land, but the storm would not let them. Jonah said, "God is angry with me, the storm will only stop if I get off the ship." The people did not want to throw Jonah overboard but they did not want to die either.

So they threw Jonah into the sea. Just then a huge fish came and swallowed Jonah whole. Jonah lived inside the big fish for three days. Jonah prayed to God. He said, "Please forgive me." .

After three days, the big fish spit Jonah onto dry land. The Lord again asked Jonah to go to Nineveh. This time, Jonah obeyed.

Jonah 1-4

THE SON OF GOD

Many prophets lived on earth after Adam. Each prophet knew that someday the Son of God would be born. The prophets testified of his birth.

Isaiah was a prophet. The Lord once told Isaiah, *"Behold, a virgin shall conceive, and bear a son, and shall call his name Immanuel."* Isaiah was happy to know the Son of God would be born on the earth. He and all of the other prophets looked forward to the day that Jesus would be born.

Isaiah 7 (Isaiah 7:14)

The New Testament

MARY

Long ago lived a righteous woman named Mary. She was chosen by Heavenly Father to be the mother of Jesus.

One day, an angel appeared to Mary. He said, "You are favored of God. You will have a special baby son. You will call him Jesus and he will be the Son of God."

After he left, Mary thought about what the angel had said. She knew this was a very important time for her.

St. Luke 1

ZACHARIAS LOSES HIS VOICE

Mary had an older cousin named Elisabeth. Elisabeth and her husband, Zacharias, wanted to have a child but they were too old. Then one day an angel appeared to Zacharias.

The angel said, “Do not fear, I am Gabriel, and I have good news.” Gabriel told Zacharias that his wife would soon have a baby son. He said they should name him John. Gabriel said, “Your son will be a special child who will someday prepare people to meet the Son of God.”

Zacharias thought Elisabeth was too old to have a baby, and did not believe the angel. So Gabriel showed Zacharias he was serious by taking away his voice. The angel said, "Your voice will return as soon as you name your baby son, John."

Elisabeth did not tell people she was having a child. But one person knew. One day her cousin Mary came to visit her. She knew Elisabeth would have a baby boy. She told Elisabeth that an angel had told her the happy news. Elisabeth and Mary felt very blessed to be a part of such miracles!

St. Luke 1

HIS NAME IS JOHN

Eight days after Elisabeth had her baby son, men came to see them. The men asked Elisabeth what they would name their son. Elisabeth said, “John.”

The men were surprised! It was their custom to name the child after the father or another relative. The men did not know anyone named John in their family.

Then they asked Zacharias, "What will you name your son?" But Zacharias still could not talk. So on a tablet he wrote, "His name is John."

Just as Zacharias finished writing this, his voice returned! This is just how the angel said it would happen. It was a very special time for Zacharias and Elisabeth. They had waited a long time for a baby and many people shared their joy. They had a big celebration with all of their friends.

St. Luke 1

MARY AND JOSEPH

Mary was engaged to a good man named Joseph when an angel visited her to say she would be Jesus' mother. She wondered, "What will Joseph think when I tell him about the angel's message." She hoped Joseph would still want to marry her.

One night while Joseph was sleeping, he had a special dream. He dreamed that he should marry Mary. He dreamed that she was the virgin told of by the prophets of old. Mary would give birth to the Son of God. And Joseph would be His earthly father.

Joseph and Mary did wed and Joseph felt blessed to be a part of such a wonderful time.

St. Matthew 1

THE FIRST CHRISTMAS

Mary and Joseph had to go to a far away land to pay their taxes. Mary would soon have her baby but she had to go anyway. Mary rode on a donkey most of the way.

One evening, they arrived in Bethlehem. All of the inns were full. They could not find a place to sleep. One innkeeper told them they could sleep in his stable with his animals. Mary and Joseph were grateful to have a covered place to sleep.

During the night, Mary had her baby. It was a healthy baby boy. He was the Son of God. They named him Jesus just as the angel said they should. Mary wrapped him in swaddling clothes and laid him in a manger. Joseph and Mary were so happy. This was a very special night.

Luke 2

THE SHEPHERDS

Shepherds watching their sheep that first Christmas night saw a new star in the sky. Angels from heaven appeared and told the shepherds that the Son of God was born. The angels told them where to find the new baby. The angels sang, *"Glory to God in the highest, and on earth peace, good will toward men."*

The shepherds hurried to Bethlehem. They found Mary and Joseph. The shepherds told them about the angel's visit.

They asked to see Jesus. They stood before the Son of God. The shepherds felt honored to be with Him. This was truly a remarkable night for the shepherds.

St. Luke 2 (Luke 2:14)

THE THREE WISE MEN

A beautiful, new star appeared in the sky the night Jesus was born. People all over the world were waiting for this sign. It was a sign that Jesus was born.

Three wise men in the East were looking for this sign. They lived far away from Bethlehem but they wanted to see the Son of God. They packed their belongings and loaded their camels and followed the new star to Bethlehem.

They rejoiced when they found Jesus. They knelt before the Son of God. They brought him precious gifts. They brought him gold, frankincense and myrrh. After their long journey, they were happy to find and worship Jesus.

St. Matthew 2

SIMEON AND ANNA

Mary and Joseph took Jesus to a temple when he was eight days old. An old man named Simeon worked at the temple. He was a good man.

God promised Simeon that he would see the Son of God before he died. After Simeon blessed Jesus, he looked at Mary and Joseph and said, "I have just held the Son of God."

Then as Mary and Joseph were leaving the temple, they passed by a woman named Anna. She spent most of her time praying and fasting at the temple. She also knew the baby was the Son of God. It was a very happy day for Simeon and Anna. They both knew they had just seen the Son of God.

St. Luke 2

MISSING!

When Jesus was twelve years old, he and his parents went to Jerusalem. They went every year for the Passover Feast. It took a whole day to walk there.

Jesus went to the temple while they were in Jerusalem. Mary and Joseph did not know that Jesus had gone to the temple alone. After they started traveling back to their home, they noticed that Jesus was missing!

Joseph and Mary were worried about their son. They hurried back to Jerusalem. After three days of searching, they finally found him in the temple. Jesus had been talking to the wise teachers. He was both learning and teaching. The wise teachers marveled at Jesus. They wondered, “How could such a young man understand so much?”

Mary asked, "Jesus, why are you here?" Jesus replied, "I am doing my Father's work." Mary did not understand him. But Jesus meant his Heavenly Father's work. Together they left the temple. And Jesus continued to grow in wisdom and in size.

St. Luke 2

JOHN THE BAPTIST

Jesus' cousin, John, grew up to be a fine young man. He started teaching people about Jesus. Some people thought John might be the Son of God. But he said, "No." He said, "I am just teaching and preparing the people to meet the real Son of God."

One day, Jesus came to John. Jesus asked John to baptize him. John did not feel worthy to baptize the Son of God. But Jesus told him that this was Heavenly Father's plan. John felt very blessed to be able to baptize Jesus.

Jesus and John went into the
Jordan River. John baptized Jesus.

When Jesus came up out of the water, they heard a quiet voice from heaven. It was Heavenly Father saying, "*This is my beloved Son, in whom I am well pleased.*"

Matthew 3 (Matthew 3:17)

A WEDDING PARTY

Jesus and his family and friends went to a wedding reception. When Jesus arrived, his mother told him that all the wine was gone. They only had water left to drink. Jesus asked for the servants to pour water into six water pots. Then Jesus turned the water into wine. He asked them to serve the drink.

The governor of the wedding was the first to have a taste. He commented that this wine was better than the wine served earlier in the day. He did not know that it was water until Jesus had turned it into wine!

St. John 2

JESUS HEALS THE BLIND

Jesus called twelve men to help him with his ministry. He called them Apostles. Their names were Peter, Andrew, James, John, Philip, Bartholomew, Simon, Matthew, James, Thomas, Thaddaeus and Judas. They traveled with Jesus from town to town teaching people about God's plan. During this time, Jesus healed many people.

One day a blind man was sitting by the roadside. He heard that Jesus was nearby. The man thought Jesus could heal his eyes so he wanted to talk to Him. The man started yelling in a loud voice to get his attention. He kept yelling louder and louder. People standing nearby told him to stop yelling. But he really wanted to meet Jesus, so he kept yelling anyway.

Jesus heard the man. He invited the man to come to him. The man hurried over to Jesus and asked him to heal his eyes so that he could see. Jesus said, *"Go thy way; thy faith hath made thee whole."* And at that moment the man's eyes were completely healed. For the first time in his life, he could see.

St. John 13, St. Mark 10 (St. Mark 10: 52)

JESUS HEALS THE DEAF

On another day when Jesus was traveling between towns, a man was brought to him. He could not hear or speak very well.

Jesus took the man away from the crowd of people. Jesus touched the man's ears and looked to heaven. Jesus said, "Be opened." Suddenly the man could hear and talk. He was completely healed. Jesus asked the man not to tell anyone about the healing. But now that the man could talk, he wanted to tell everyone about this great miracle!

St. Mark 7

JESUS RAISES THE DEAD

One day when Jesus was walking with a large group of people, a man came to him. He said he only had one daughter. She was twelve years old and she was dying. He asked Jesus to save her life.

Jesus went to the man's daughter. The people sitting by her were crying. They told Jesus that she had already died. But Jesus said, "She is not dead, but only sleeping."

Jesus asked to be alone with the girl. He held her hand and said, "Maid, arise." And the young girl came back to life. Jesus told her family to feed her and asked them not to tell anyone of this miracle. But the more Jesus told people not to tell, the more they wanted to spread the good news. Many people were learning about his great power.

St. Luke 8:54

A SICK WOMAN'S FAITH

On another day while Jesus was walking with a crowd of people, he felt someone touch his robe. He asked, "Who touched me?" His friends said, "There were many people following you. It could have been anyone." But Jesus said he felt that he had healed someone.

A woman behind Jesus fell to the ground. She said, "It was I!" The woman had been ill for a long time and she believed that if she could just touch Jesus, then she would be well. Jesus told her not to be afraid. He said, "*Daughter, be of good comfort; thy faith hath made thee whole; go in peace.*" The woman was so happy! She was completely healed just by touching his robe!

St. Luke 8 (St. Luke 8:48)

THE TEN LEPERS

One day when Jesus was walking, he saw a group of men. There were ten of them. They all had leprosy. Leprosy is a very painful illness that never goes away. Leprosy spreads easily from one person to another. So these ten men had to live away from everyone else. They were all very sad.

The men called to Jesus when they saw him. They asked him to heal their illness. Jesus said, “Go see the priests.” By the time the ten lepers found the priests, they were completely healed.

One leper returned to Jesus. He said, “Thank you for healing me!” Jesus asked, “Where are the other nine who were healed?” The man did not know. He said, “Only I have come back to thank you.”

Jesus reminds us to always thank other people when they do something kind for us.

St. Luke 17

MARY AND MARTHA

In a small village lived a woman named Martha. She and her sister, Mary, invited Jesus to eat with them. Martha wanted Mary to help her cook, serve and clean up. But Mary was busy listening to Jesus. She was learning about God.

Martha was not happy. She was angry with Mary. She complained to Jesus. But Jesus said, "Martha do not be angry. Mary is learning about important things. Soon I will leave and then you can clean up." Jesus taught Martha that it is important to learn about God whenever we have the chance.

St. Matthew 10

FIVE LOAVES OF BREAD AND TWO FISH

Many people followed Jesus. Some wanted to be healed. Others wanted to learn about God.

Once while Jesus was teaching a large group of people, his disciples asked if they should send everyone home. It was time for dinner. Jesus did not want to send them away. He asked his disciples, “How much food do we have?” They told Jesus they only had five loaves of bread and two fish.

Jesus told his disciples to ask the people to stay and eat. He asked the people to sit on the grassy hillside in big groups. Jesus blessed the food. After he blessed the food, there was enough bread and fish for all of the people. Jesus fed five thousand people with only five loaves of bread and two fish!

St. Mark 6

JESUS WALKS ON WATER

One evening, the disciples were in a fishing boat. They were trying to row to shore but it was very windy and the ship would not move. Jesus saw his disciples out at sea. He wanted them to come to shore, but they could not see him. So Jesus decided to walk out to the boat.

Jesus walked right on top of the water! As he approached the boat, his disciples thought it must be a ghost moving towards them. But Jesus called to them. He said, *"Be of good cheer; it is I; be not afraid."* His disciples were so surprised!

Peter asked if he could walk out to Jesus. Peter tried walking on the water. After a few steps, a big gust of wind came. It frightened Peter. He started to sink into the water. Peter called to Jesus to help him.

Jesus put out his hand and pulled Peter out of the water. They walked on the water together. They walked to the boat. The disciples marveled at Jesus. They said, "You really are the Son of God."

St. Matthew (St. Matthew 14:27)

THE GOOD SAMARITAN

Jesus was teaching a group of people one day. He said, "We should love our neighbors as ourselves." A man in the group asked, "Who is our neighbor?" Jesus answered with a special story called a parable. A parable is a story that we can learn from. This parable is about a Good Samaritan.

Jesus said, "A man was traveling to a far off town. He was attacked by robbers and was left lying in the dirt. Then along came a priest. The priest did not stop to help him. Then came another man. But he did not stop either. Then came a stranger from a distant land called Samaria. The Samaritan stopped to help the man in trouble."

Then Jesus asked, “Who was the neighbor?” The man replied, “The Samaritan.” Jesus said, “We should all be like the Samaritan. We should always help other people.”

St. Luke 10

THE SERMON ON THE MOUNT

Large groups of people followed Jesus. One day Jesus went high on the side of a mountain so everyone could see and hear him. He gave a sermon this day.

He taught the people many things. He taught them how to live, pray, and help one another and how to become perfect. Jesus said, "If we do these things we will be happy and we will return to live with our Father in Heaven."

St. Matthew 5

A HAPPY DAY

Jesus and his disciples walked to many cities. They told people about God's plan. Many people followed Jesus. They knew he was the Son of God.

One day when Jesus and his disciples were returning to Jerusalem, someone brought a donkey for Jesus to ride on. The people following Jesus laid down their coats on the ground for the donkey to walk on. Other people put down leaves and palms from trees to line the road. They did this to show Jesus how much they loved him.

As Jesus rode through the city gates, the people cheered. Strangers watching his entry asked, "Who is this man?" His followers replied, *"This is the prophet of Nazareth of Galilee."* And the large group of people surrounding him cheered, "Hosanna, hosanna"! These people loved Jesus very much.

St. Matthew (St. Matthew 21:10)

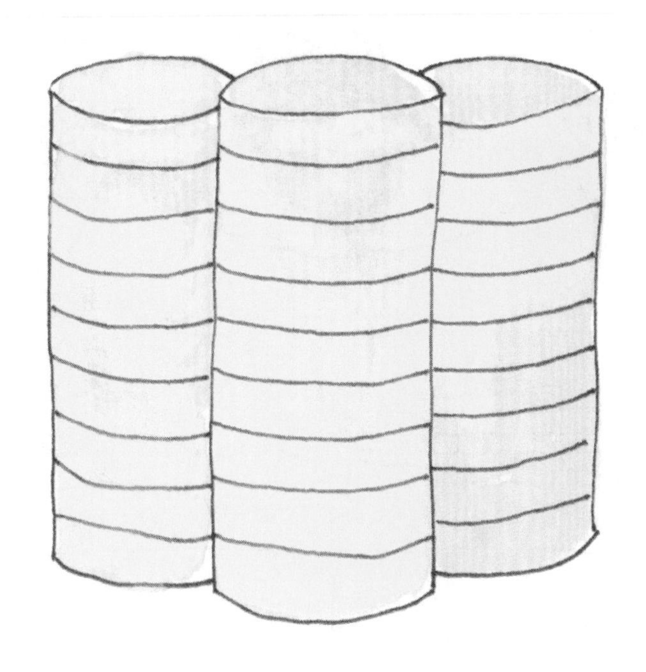

GREEDY MEN

After Jesus returned to Jerusalem, he went to the temple. He was surprised and angry by what he saw there. People were inside the temple buying and selling animals and charging money for the Passover Feast. The temple was not meant to be a marketplace! The temple was a special place to worship God.

Jesus wanted the greedy men to leave the temple. Jesus said, "*My house shall be called the house of prayer; but ye have made it a den of thieves.*" Then Jesus threw their tables over and sent the men away. Now the people could come to the temple and worship in peace.

St. Matthew (St. Matthew 21:13)

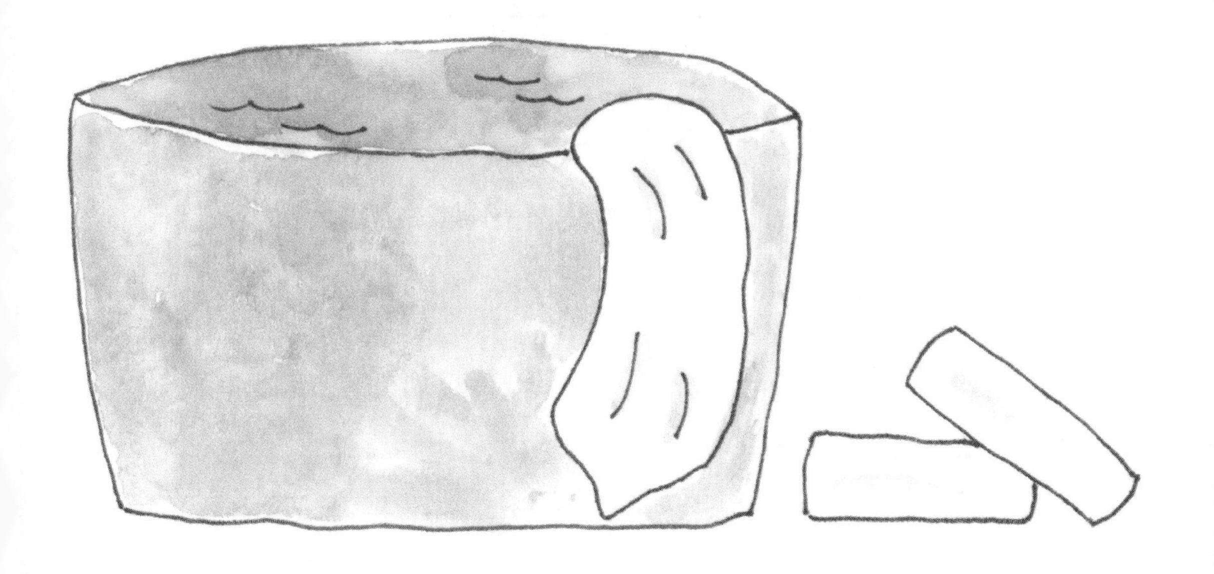

THE FIRST SACRAMENT

Jesus knew he would die soon. It was part of Heavenly Father's plan. He met with his twelve disciples for a special dinner. Before they started, Jesus washed all of his disciple's feet. It was his way of showing his love for them. One of his disciples, Peter, did not want the Son of God to wash his feet! But Jesus insisted.

Jesus told his disciples that they should always love one another. Then he took a piece of bread and blessed it and broke it and gave it to his disciples. He also gave them a drink and said, “You should remember me each week by partaking of bread and wine.” This was the first sacrament.

Then Jesus said, "One of you will betray me." They asked, "Which of us will betray you"? He gave a piece of food to the disciple. It was Judas. Judas left and told Jewish soldiers where to find Jesus. Then the soldiers gave Judas money.

St. Matthew 26

FOR US!

After eating, Jesus and his disciples went to a beautiful garden. Jesus asked his friends to stay with him. Jesus found a private place to pray. He asked Heavenly Father to allow him to pay for our sins.

He prayed a long time. He suffered for all of our sins. It was painful for Jesus to do this but he knew it was important. His friends fell asleep. So Jesus kept praying alone. Jesus suffered this night so that we could return to live with Heavenly Father. He did this just for us!

St. Matthew 25-26

THE SADDEST DAY

Early in the morning, Jewish soldiers came looking for Jesus. Judas told them where to find him. Jesus went peacefully with the soldiers. There was a trial. The wicked rulers did not like Jesus saying he was the Son of God. The leaders led Jesus away. They crucified him. Jesus died on the cross. This was a very sad day for the followers of Jesus.

St. Matthew 25-26

THE FIRST EASTER

A friend of Jesus took his body and laid it in a special tomb. He rolled a big rock in front of it. Mary, another friend of Jesus, came to the tomb three days later. She was surprised to see that the rock had been rolled away. She looked inside. Jesus was not there! There were two angels sitting in the tomb. They said, "Jesus has risen."

A man from behind her asked, "Why are you crying?" Mary said, "Jesus is gone!" But the voice said, "Do not be sad, for I live." Mary looked behind her. It was Jesus! He was alive! This was the most important day for us. Because Jesus came back to life, we will too. We will all live again!

St. John 20

HE LIVES!

Jesus went to see his disciples after His resurrection. They were surprised to see him! They had not understood what it meant that Jesus would die but live again. They were very happy to be with him once more. Jesus asked them to be missionaries. He said, "You should tell people about the gospel and then baptize them."

After Jesus said goodbye, he ascended up to heaven. His disciples watched him leave. They looked towards the sky for a long time after Jesus left.

Then two angels came and stood by the disciples. The angels asked, “Why are you still looking up at the sky? Jesus has gone to heaven. Someday He will come back just as you have seen him leave.” The disciples felt so happy. They were grateful to have known Jesus.

St. Matthew 28, The Acts 1

A CHANGE OF HEART

Many people still believed in Jesus after He left. They were called Christians. Some people who did not believe in Jesus were mean to the Christians. One mean man was named Saul. The Christians feared Saul. He did not want Christians to live.

One day Jesus appeared to Saul when he was traveling between cities. Saul saw a bright light surrounding his body. Saul fell to the ground. Jesus asked, "Why are you hurting the Christians? Do you not know that they are doing my work?"

Saul could not see after Jesus left. His friends had to lead him to the next city. A Christian man was waiting for Saul. He blessed him so that he could see again. Saul now knew he was wrong for hurting the Christians. He felt terrible for the harm he had caused. He decided not to be mean anymore. He changed his name to Paul and he decided to be a missionary! He wanted to tell people about Jesus.

Acts 9

HEAVEN ON EARTH

There once lived a Christian man named John. He was an apostle to Jesus. John was put in prison because he believed in Jesus. He was alone in prison. The Lord came to him and showed him the future.

John saw a busy, changing world. He saw plagues and wars and wild weather. He saw that Christ's church was on the earth. And he saw that Jesus would come again to live on the earth.

The second time, Jesus will come down from the sky in heavenly glory! This will be a joyful day for all the good people living on the earth. It will be a very special time when Jesus comes again!

Revelation 1-22

About the Author/Illustrator

Laura Lee Blocher Rostrom is a native of Seattle, Washington, and a graduate of Brigham Young University. She currently lives in Westchester County, New York, with her husband, Dean and their three children. This is Laura's second published book. *My Book of Mormon Storybook* was a bestseller and is becoming a family classic.

We hope you enjoy *My Bible Storybook* for many years to come! To order a copy of this storybook or *My Book of Mormon Storybook*, please contact CFI (Cedar Fort, Inc.) at any of the following:

Phone: 1-800-SKY-BOOK (759-2665)
Facsimile: 1-800-489-9432
e-mail: skybook@itsnet.com